Me Again!

(and Charlie)

↖ me!

A SNOWY STATE OF MIND

↗ Charlie!

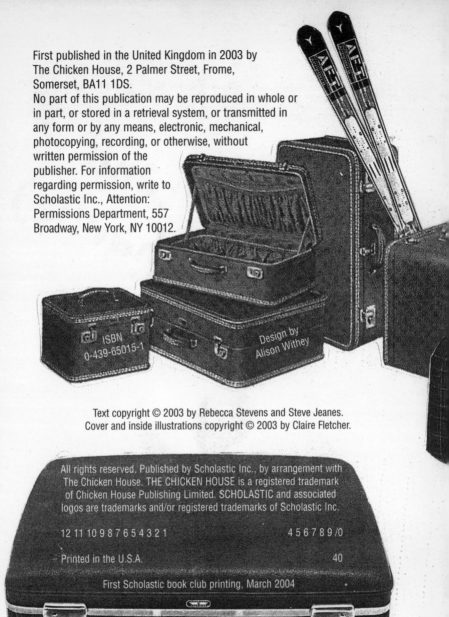

First published in the United Kingdom in 2003 by
The Chicken House, 2 Palmer Street, Frome,
Somerset, BA11 1DS.

ISBN
0-439-65015-1

Design by
Alison Withey

12 11 10 9 8 7 6 5 4 3 2 1   4 5 6 7 8 9 /0

Printed in the U.S.A.   40

First Scholastic book club printing, March 2004

Me Again!

(and Charlie)

A SNOWY STATE OF MIND

Janet Fish and Charlie Wells
Typed by Rebecca Stevens and Steve Jeanes

SCHOLASTIC INC.

New York Toronto London Auckland Sydney
Mexico City New Delhi Hong Kong Buenos Aires

THANKS TO:
Everyone who read our first book
— you're THE BIZ!

And everyone who didn't but who's got this one,
cos you're The Biz too! (Especially if you get the
first one next!)

My mum for . . . well, everything, really.

Wizzo, for being the coolest dad in the world,
wherever he is in it.

Tiffani, cos she's my best friend (even though she
doesn't exist).

My sister, Dee (HA!), for services to the lip-gloss
industry.

Deirdre, Charlie's mum, for being able to drive a
bus, and her wacko hippie mate, Gandolfo, for
lending it to her.

Geri, Charlie's four-year-old sister. (She doesn't
really deserve it, but I don't want to be the next
person she bites.)

Johnny Ho, who wrote the weird titles for the
chapters, and who is probably an alien.

Daisy Micklepage, for always making a complete pratt of herself in public.

Those old crusties Rebecca Stevens and Steve Jeanes, who typed it for us again. I mean, it's really good of them, but I do wish they'd GET A LIFE!

My art teacher, Claire Fletcher, who thought the BOTTOMFLIES idea was pretty good really.

Prince William, because he's still GORGEOUS!

Charlie, I suppose. Well, he did do a few more bits and pieces.

Janet

(Author & Artist)

Me

Charlie

Chapter One

Beware the shadow of envy. It follows in the footsteps of good fortune

Well.

I DID think that me and Charlie were going to be really good friends.

But I was wrong.

We're not going to be really good friends. We're not even going to be really bad friends. Or really good enemies. We're not going to be anything at all. Not anymore.

Because I hate him.

I do.

I hate his nose and his hair and his big square teeth and the way his left eye sometimes does this

1

weird twitchy thing when he's looking at you. I hate his room and his handwriting and his stupid stupid football. I hate THAT most of all — the mud and the boots and the boys running about and shouting "over 'ere, mate!" at each other and the dads getting all red in the face and cheering when their sons score a goal. What's that all about? Eh? I mean, what is that all about? When there are little children in other countries starving to death through not having enough to eat, how can you get all excited just because some stupid boy has kicked a stupid ball between two stupid posts on some muddy playing field somewhere in England?

Eh?

When I leave school I'm going to get a job Helping Humanity (as well as being a world-famous artist, of course). I'll organize food packages for those children and help build them schools and hospitals and stuff. Or I could teach them all about intensive farming so they'd have loads and loads of really cheap chickens to eat. I know they're not all that healthy (Mum says they're chock-a-block full of chemicals and stuff), but if you've got nothing else, I expect you'd be glad to have them. Or maybe I'll just be President of the World and pass a law making it illegal for some people to have loads and loads of money while others don't have any at all. That might be easier actually.

Anyway.

Whatever I do, it's going to be for the Good of Humanity.

Unlike Charlie.

He wants to be a football player.

How sick is that?

Janet keeps saying how she wants to travel the world and help deprived children and all that. Then she gives me this funny stare as though that's supposed to mean something to me. I'm not stupid. I know exactly what she means. She means she's decided not to be a famous artist after all. She wants to be a PRINCESS. Not because she likes doing princessy things, like walking sideways and waving at the same time or keeping the bad hatmakers in business. She wants to be a princess because she's got a THING about Prince William.

Ha! As if Prince William would fancy someone with braces on her teeth who snorts lemonade out her nose when she's laughing. Anyway, who's ever heard of a Princess Janet? The Queen would go bananas.

Mind you, I'm not telling her. I'm not that daft. NEVER tell a girl she's living in la-la land. Not if you ever want to walk again.

Or play football . . .

I don't know if I've mentioned it yet, but guess who made the school football team?

CHARLIE WELLS, superstar offense player, that's who!!!!

The reasons I hate Charlie are:

1. He wants to be a football player when he leaves school instead of helping humanity.

2. He said he reckoned Prince William was a "bit of a der-brain".

3. He's going on holiday to France when we break up from school.

He's going on holiday to France!

How unfair is that?

I've never been to France.

I've never been abroad.

I have been on holiday though. When Dad still lived with us, we had a week once in this really amazing place called Cromer.

It's on the coast, and even though there's not an incredible amount to do there and it is usually quite freezing cold and windy, we had a FANTASTIC time. Mum and Dad did spend quite a lot of the holiday arguing and Dee was in a major sulk because Mum wouldn't let her have her belly button pierced and I spent most of my time lying in my bunk bed trying not to scratch because I had chicken pox, but it was just so great to be on holiday as a family that none of us cared!

But it's not QUITE as good as going to France, is it?

FRANCE!

Land of croissants! And artists! And haute cuisine! (That means "high kitchen" for anybody who doesn't speak French.) And people kissing all the time whether they like each other or not! (They practically invented snogging in France, you know. Why d'you think they call it FRENCH kissing? It was probably some French bloke back in the eighteenth century who discovered that sucking somebody else's teeth was really good fun. I've never tried it myself, of course, but if it was invented in France then it must be OK.)

And that's not all, actually.

I don't hate Charlie just because he's going to France.

I hate him because he's going SNOWBOARDING in France.

How sick-making is that?

Charlie is going snowboarding in France and I've got to stay at home on my own in a cold, damp flat, watching TV with the curtains closed and nothing to eat but cold baked beans for the entire holiday. . . .

sad

Man, am I amped! Can't wait to hit that kicker and jib the pipe. Yeah!

Well, erm, I might be if I understood what it meant. This is the other great thing happening as well as the football. We're going on a trip! Me, Deirdre, and the

Thing That Bites (my sister, Geri)! We're going in Pegasus the bus! To France! Brilliant! And I'm going snowboarding in the Alps!!!! Cool, or what? Am I amped!!

I think it means excited (amped, that is). I bought a snowboarding mag to get some idea of how to do it, but it was just a load of people talking in this funny language. The photos were totally fantastic though. I can't wait. Once I've got the language right, the rest'll be dead easy, I can tell. I'll be one of the dudes in no time. Shame Janet isn't coming, but it's not really a girl thing. There's got to be other stuff in France that girls like though. Cakes or something.

Of course, the big problem with France (don't get me wrong, I'm still dead excited about going) is that they all speak French. And I don't. I'm a "stupid, inattentive, English yob" according to Mr. McTavish, my French teacher. McTavish has been giving me a really hard time since he heard I was going on holiday to his beloved France. He keeps telling me how nobody's going to bother to talk to an ignorant little kid who doesn't speak a word of "le bow fronsay," as he calls it. I don't care. I'm going to get back at him. He's goal-keeper in the annual Teachers vs. Kids game on

Saturday, and Charlie Wells, superplayer, is going to make him eat the shorts of shame in front of the whole school!

To: Tiffani
From: Janet
Re: Easter vacation!

hey Tiff, what are you up to over the break? You'll never guess what I'M doing.

I'm going snowboarding in France!

How cool is that?

....

I'm doing it again, aren't I? Making out things are better than they are, I mean. Why don't I just admit it. I'm not going to France and I don't hate Charlie. I'm jealous. I'm jealous because he's going to France and I'm not. There, I said it.

I'm jealous.

Jealous jealous jealous.

I'm SO JEALOUS I COULD SCREAM
ARGGGG GHH HHH!
ARGG GGG HH H HH!
YUGH HH H H H H!
YURGH H H H HHH!

WEEARGHARWOOO!

EEE E E E E E E E K!

It's no good. I'm still jealous.

And I still hate Charlie. . . .

Isn't it just so cool when everything's going right for you? You want all your mates to join in and have a good time too. It would have been great if Janet or Johnny could have come with us, so I asked Deirdre if I could bring a friend along. She was a bit funny when I asked her though. She's going through one of her weirdy phases. Keeps looking at all these art books and going all misty and out of it. I don't know what it is with these women who like "Art." You don't know what's going through their heads half the time. Her and Janet are just the same like that. Woolly. They could both do with some sport. That would wake them up. You can't go off on one when a big dirty goalkeeper's clattering into your chest with his bony great elbows, or a midfield general's crushing your ankle with his size thirteens. Sport's good for you!

Anyway, so far the answer's No, but I'll have another try when Deirdre's back on the planet.

You wouldn't think things could get any worse, would you?

Well, they have.

Do you remember in my last book (my last book! How cool does that sound!) how I told you about the dreaded DAISY MICKLEPAGE and how horrible she is and how me and Charlie got our revenge with the Great Blue Bottomflies incident? (If you don't remember, or haven't read it, it doesn't matter. All you need to know is that she's the most annoying, snotty, showy-off pig in the entire universe and that we HATE her. Oh, yes, and go out and buy the book!)

Well.

You'd think the Blue Bottomflies
thing would've shut her up,
wouldn't you? Anybody normal would want
to go into hiding for about a year and only
come out when they were sure everybody had
forgotten about it.

Not her. Not Miss "we go to our villa in
Tuscany for our vacations every year actually"
Daisy Micklepage. She's walking round like
she's Madonna or somebody with her nose
in the air and this superior look on her face
just because she got her picture in the local
paper! How sad is that? She was in some
stupid little show (she goes to Drama Club
after school on Thursdays "because she's
such a brilliant actress") and they took a
photo of the cast and put it in the paper
because they haven't got anything better to
fill up their sad little pages! And now she's
going round saying that the photographer
said the camera really loved her (whatever
that means) and she's going to be a SUPER-
MODEL!

Well, somebody had to set her straight, didn't they?

So I told her she didn't look much like a supermodel to me. She looked more like a stupid blond pig in a wig.

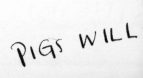

So she did this really annoying tossy thing with her hair and said I was just jealous because nobody would ever put MY picture in the paper unless it was to advertise a horror film. And all her friends laughed. Which made me so mad that I couldn't think of anything to say. So they flounced off, smirking and tossing their stupid hair about, while I just stood there.

But I'll get my own back.

I always do.

PIGS WILL

15

Chapter Two

Sadness brings a new direction

Jealousy's a funny thing, isn't it? I mean, when something nice happens to someone you like (and I do like Charlie, honest), you ought to be pleased. But you hardly ever are. You just wish something horrible would happen to them and take the nice thing away.

SCREECH!

Or is that just me?

I do feel a BIT better actually. I'm not saying
I'm exactly overjoyed about Charlie going on
holiday, but I have stopped hoping something
horrible will happen so he has to stay at home.
Something like his mum losing her job or his
sister getting knocked down by a bus. Or him
coming down with a killer disease that brings
him out in huge green pus-filled boils so he
has to stay in bed the whole time. I don't hope
any of that will happen to him now. Which
must mean that I'm becoming a Better
Person.

Which is good.

Part of me's always wanted to become a
Better Person. I mean, there's no point in
Helping Humanity if you're just doing it so
everybody'll go "Wow, isn't she great? What a
good good good good person, I wish I could be
like her," is there? Because then you're just
being good to show off, not because you truly
want to help people. Like Princess Diana (she
was Prince William's mum and she was always

17

off Helping the Poor and Cuddling the Sick and digging up land mines with her bare hands and stuff. Unlike SOME members of the so-called Royal Family who are far more interested in chasing defenseless little foxes round the country and sunbathing with topless models than in Doing Good. Prince William takes after his mum, obviously — you can tell he's a really nice person just by looking at him).

Anyway. I'm feeling so much of a Better Person that I think I'll go round and see Charlie after tea and make friends and tell him how happy I am that he's been offered this wonderful opportunity to travel to a sophisticated foreign country like France where they're into things like ART and FINE FOOD and SUCKING EACH OTHER'S TEETH and broaden his narrow little football-obsessed mind.

the rest of the world

That'll show him.

Charlie's Brain.

The French are, of course, famous for one thing —
football. They were World Champions once (they won
the first World Cup I ever saw). Not like McTavish. The
only thing he'll ever be World Champion of is being
a fat and smelly slug. Still, if I was going to score
against His Sliminess, I was going to need some
practice.

I couldn't practice on my own though, so I got Johnny
to help by standing in for Mr. McTavish as goalie.
Johnny isn't much good at being a goalie. He's all the
wrong shape for a start. Everything's too short. His
arms, his legs, his eyesight. But he never gives up. It
gave me a chance to try all kinds of different shots. I
scored twenty-three goals, no probs! Maybe I should
have let him wear his glasses.

Guess what?

He wasn't there.

Tuesday's only his stupid football night, isn't it?

His mum was there, though. Weirdre Deirdre.
And she was acting even more weird than usual.
What happened was this. The door to their

19

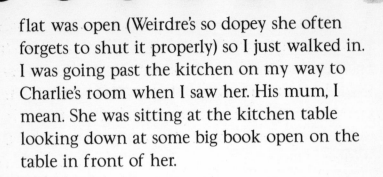

flat was open (Weirdre's so dopey she often forgets to shut it properly) so I just walked in. I was going past the kitchen on my way to Charlie's room when I saw her. His mum, I mean. She was sitting at the kitchen table looking down at some big book open on the table in front of her.

And she was crying.

Not big loud boo-hooey type crying, but soft, snuffly, trying-to-wipe-your-nose-on-the-back-of-your-hand-and-failing-miserably-because-the-tears-keep-on-coming-and-coming-and-coming-type crying. Grown-up crying.

Well.

You can imagine how I felt. I mean, it's embarrassing enough seeing your OWN mum cry, but someone else's . . .

Ew.

Just thinking about it makes me go all hot and shuddery.

20

So I was just about to sneak out and leave her to it when I remembered about being a Better Person. Princess Diana wouldn't have left a poor woman crying on her own in a kitchen, even if she did have purple hair and snot all over her sweater (the woman, I mean, not Princess Diana).

So I went in.

I felt really stupid at first because I didn't know what to do. Princess Diana would probably just have put her arms round her and hugged her (once she'd cleared the area of land mines of course) and let her leak snot and tears all over her sweater, but I wasn't about to do that. Not JUST because I was wearing my new top (it's Board Babes, actually. You know, with the sleeves a different color from the body?) but . . . well, I couldn't. So I just stood there making sort of sympathetic little huffing sounds through my nose until she looked up and saw me.

Well.

Any normal person would've been pretty
embarrassed if someone had walked in and
found them all puffy-eyed and red in the face
like that, but Deirdre's not normal. She just
wiped her eyes with the back of her hand,
blew her nose on her skirt, and told me to sit
down and have a look at this book she had in
front of her.

So I did.

And do you know what?

It was amazing.

Amazing!!!

After I'd scored my hundredth goal I decided to call it
a day. Johnny, being Johnny, wanted to carry on.

"Charlie, I'm absolutely, definitely, one hundred per-
cent certain I'm going to save at least one shot!" he
said. But as he was talking to the sweatshirt I'd hung
on the corner post at the time, there wasn't really
much point in going on.

So we went back to his place, which was great
because he's got the best collection of snowboarding

magazines ever. He's never been snowboarding of course, but he likes the pictures because of all the snow. He says it reminds him of the "universal one-ness of everything" — whatever that means. I've learned not to ask. He's always coming up with stuff like that. It was great to thumb through the magazines. This time next month, I thought, that'll be me!

Deirdre's book was filled with pictures of the most incredible paintings I've ever seen in my entire life. They weren't paintings OF anything, in fact they were quite splodgy and all-over-the-place and crazy-looking, but they looked sort of ALIVE. The colors seemed to move and squirm and wiggle and twitch like germs under a microscope except not yucky like that, they were beautiful and sort of . . . funny. Yes, funny. They made you want to smile just to look at them. It's hard to explain. All I know is that I loved those paintings so much my tummy hurt. Then Deirdre explained that they were done by a quite famous artist she once knew (!)

and that they were called ACTION paintings. Which means that the artist wouldn't use a brush to paint them, that'd be way too ordinary. He'd just get this really HUGE canvas (some of the paintings were as big as a double-decker bus, Deirdre said) and CHUCK paint at it or DRIBBLE it out of a watering can or STOMP on it with his boots or RIDE A BIKE through it or take off all his clothes and ROLL ABOUT IN IT TOTALLY NAKED! Just like I was going to do with my Blue Bottomflies in the school hall (except for the totally naked bit, obviously)! I was an Action Painter all along and I never even knew it.

Well.

When Deirdre explained about the paintings I forgot all about being a Better Person like Princess Diana and growing up to Help Humanity.

I'm going to be an Action Painter and make pictures like the ones in Deirdre's book.

You wait.

Chapter Three

Good news is sometimes bad news in disguise

Deffo

So.

As soon as I got back I decided to do some Action Painting straightaway. And this time nobody was going to stop me. Not Charlie, not anyone. Just think, if it wasn't for him, I would've finished my Blue Bottomflies mural and would probably have been a seriously famous artist by this time, with my picture in all the papers and a whole book written about me like that bloke of Deirdre's.

Anyway.

I was lucky. Mum was out and Dee was holed up in her room with some boring friend, so I had the place pretty much to myself.

The first problem was what to do the painting

At least I have friends, unlike some people

ON. I didn't have any canvas, obviously, but I found some rolls of old wallpaper in the back of the hall cupboard. I spread them all out on the floor of the living room and stuck five sheets together with sticky tape to make one piece that was really ginormous. Then I got some red emulsion paint that was left over from decorating the loo, prized the lid off with the bread knife, and gave it a good stir.

Then I looked around for something to apply it with. That was the tricky bit. I would've liked a bike or some other sort of vehicle so I could just sploosh a lot of paint down on the paper and then RIDE through it, making big wizzy patterns with the wheels. But we haven't got one and I couldn't face going next door and borrowing Charlie's skateboard in case Deirdre had gone back into weepy mode and I'd have to do my Princess Diana act again. So I didn't know what to do. And then I remembered what Deirdre had said about Action Painters using their BODIES to apply the paint.

Well.

I had to give it a try, didn't I?

So.

I stripped off all my clothes, wrapped myself up in plastic wrap (well, I wasn't going to do it COMPLETELY naked, was I?) and then dolloped a big load of lovely gloopy red paint onto my "canvas."

Then I sat down in it.

It felt really weird at first. I crawled around for a bit, making prints with my feet and hands (like potato prints at primary school), and that looked quite good, but I thought a real Action Painter would use her WHOLE body. So I gritted my teeth, lay down, and started to roll (I had to be careful to avoid the bread knife, which I'd forgotten to put away, of course). It felt really

28

cold and sticky even through the plastic wrap, so as I rolled about I couldn't help making these little noises (like when you go into the sea and it's really cold and the waves keep getting higher and higher up your body):

OOOCH!

OW!

YARGHHH!

EEK!

And that was when Mum came in.

When I got home, the door was open as usual. I'd borrowed one of the snowboarding mags from Johnny, and I still had my head in it when I walked into the kitchen. Deirdre was thumbing through one of those stupid big expensive art books she likes so much, so I just dropped my dirty football gear on the kitchen table and went to my room.

I didn't realize I wasn't alone at first. I'd kicked off my shoes and laid back on the bed with the magazine before I heard the first evil growl. I sat up with a start, not sure if I'd really heard anything. The room's quite dark cos I like to keep the curtains closed. I peered into all the murky corners for a minute but couldn't see anything, so I relaxed again. The moment I did, there it was again, that familiar muffled snarl. I was sure I'd heard it this time, so I leaped off the bed and started pulling furniture around to see where it had come from. I hate it when Geri gets into my room. She always either gets herself horribly stuck somewhere or destroys something I treasure. In the past she's managed to sit on a model plane, eat a whole regiment of plastic soldiers, cover my shin pads with marmalade, and get herself trapped in the gap between the mattress and the wall so it took the two of us almost half an hour to get her out.

I checked the mattress first this time, but there was only the crust of a ham-and-pineapple pizza left over from my last birthday. I called her name and got the evil snuffling again in reply but couldn't work out where it was coming from, so I decided to pull the curtains and let in some light.

One of the curtains opened OK, but when I grabbed the other one, I let it go immediately. It was all soggy. The muffled snarling was closer. I looked up and there she was, hanging on to the top of the curtain by her teeth like some crazy, peanut-butter-covered bat. All the way up the side of the curtain were wet semicircles. It looked as though she'd managed to climb the thing just by biting her way up. Absolutely impossible, you'd have thought, but I've learned not to take anything for granted with Geri. The laws of biology and physics don't seem to apply to her. As long as it's annoying, she can do it. It doesn't matter whether it's impossible or not.

I grabbed hold of her and began to tug. The growling started immediately, followed by an unpleasant ripping noise.

Mum took it quite well actually. After she'd stopped screaming she said that she was going round to Deirdre's for a drink or three and that she didn't want to find a spot of paint on anything when she got back. Including me.

Well.

That was the first problem. I managed to clear away the wallpaper all right (there wasn't TOO much paint on the carpet underneath) and got most of it off my skin under the shower but there was just NO WAY I could get the paint out of my hair. I decided that the only thing to do was get the kitchen scissors and give myself a really cool haircut. I'd seen this style I liked on the website where I got my top (can't wait to have a credit card of my own so I can order LOADS of stuff), so I decided to get it up onscreen and copy it.

Well.

I was halfway through the haircut when I remembered I hadn't checked my e-mails. I always check them every day in case there's something from Dad, so I decided to leave my hair (which was already looking pretty amazing) and do that first.

And guess what?

Here's Dee a few years ago - ha-ha!

There was an e-mail.

And it was from
my dad.

And it contained the worst news I
have ever had in my entire life.

It always takes ages to separate Geri from something
she's got her teeth into. I finally managed it, though,
with the loss of only half a curtain. Then, holding her at
arm's length and out of reach of any chewable
objects, I marched her back to the kitchen.

It really must have taken ages, because Deirdre was
no longer on her own. Janet's mum had snuck in while
I'd been wrestling with the Thing That Bites. There
was a bottle of wine on the table and the pair of them
had that shifty look in their eyes as though I'd caught
them trading enemy secrets. They both smiled and
Janet's mum said hello, but I could tell they wanted to
be left alone. Well, that was fine by me. What mothers
talk about between themselves is a complete mystery,
though wine always seems to play an important part in

it. I dumped Geri in front of Deirdre so she could have the pleasure of trying to get half a curtain out of her mouth and reminded her that the Teachers/Kids game was on Saturday, in two days' time, and that she'd promised to come.

Deirdre looked at Kate with one of those adults' secret club looks, then turned to me and smiled.

"Of course, I'm coming. Just as long as nothing comes up. I wouldn't let you down."

I knew at that moment she was going to let me down. Probably to do a crucial bit of shopping or something. That's mothers for you. Say one thing, do another, and all the time thinking how clever they are to have got away with it. I wish I had a dad. I bet he'd tell me the truth all the time, and when he said he'd come to watch me play for my team, he'd really come.

To: Janet
From: Wizzo
Subject: my love life

hey gorgeous have i got news for you
guess what?

your old dad has only got himself a GIRL-
FRIEND!!!!!!!

whatdja reckon to that then?

her name's BEEBEE and she's a student nurse
and she's clever and funny and we get on like a
house on fire (oh and she's quite a babe an' all!)

wot's more she seems to think yr old man is the
beez kneez!

who can believe it eh?

stand by with that bridesmaid dress, gorgeous —
you never know when it's gonna come in handy!

love
yr old dad
mad, sad, bad
wizzo x :)

ps seriously sweetheart she is dead nice and i
can't wait for you to meet her

w x

And JANET isn't?!!! Dee

So my dad was getting married. And that wasn't all. He was getting married to a girl called BEEBEE (and I thought DEE was a sad name! I mean, I know Janet's not exactly EXTRAORDINARY but at least it doesn't make me sound like a brain-dead Barbie doll) who was probably young enough to be his daughter and would stop him having anything to do with me because she couldn't stand the fact that he loved me so much. And he'd go along with it because he was so blinded by her stupid blond hair and shiny white teeth that he couldn't think straight. And when they were married she'd want to have a baby straight-away because those types of women always do and it would probably be a boy who'd be really really good at playing the guitar and Dad would be over the moon about it all and would go completely soft in the head and forget all about me forever and ever amen.

36

And it would be like I'd never had a dad at all.

I was in the living room with my snowboarding mag when Janet's mum left. Her and Deirdre were whispering and giggling together about something, and they went right out into the hall to carry on out of earshot. I couldn't make out what they were saying. Sometimes I really hate mothers.

Finally, Deirdre came back and threw herself on the sofa and said, "Well, that's taken care of." I asked her what, but she just grimaced at the sound of a cutlery drawer crashing to the floor and shot off back to the kitchen. She came back clutching Geri and trying to make her let go of a rolling pin she'd taken a liking to.

"You know, Charlie, I'm really glad you and Janet are friends. That makes it all just perfect," she started, staring blankly into space as the Thing That Bites tried to wriggle away from her grip, "and I get along so well with Kate. Yes, it's perfect, absolutely perfect." And she stared off into her dreamworld again.

I was about to ask her what she meant and to bring up the business of the game on Saturday again when Geri managed to slip from her grasp and brought the rolling pin down on my knee with an almighty crunch. After that I was too busy wiping my eyes and trying not to be sick to remember what I'd wanted to say.

I was still staring at the e-mail when Mum came in. At first she started shouting about what on earth had I done to my lovely hair but then she saw what I was looking at.

Well.

She sat down on the bed and went all quiet and peculiar. Then she looked at me and said it was probably Dad just being daft as usual and to try not to worry too much. But deep down I could tell she was nearly as upset as me, so I crawled onto her lap (the last time I did that was when I was about six and a half — I am SO past that now) and we just stayed there for a bit both thinking in our own heads.

And then she sort of shook herself and said she had a bit of news that she knew would cheer me up no end.

She'd gotten me a baby-sitting job!

Yeah, well, I know it's not as good as, like, going on holiday to FRANCE or something, but it was still pretty good. I've been wanting to do baby-sitting for ages because it sounds so easy. You get paid loads of money to go round to somebody else's house when they're not there, eat their food, rummage through their cupboards, read their private mail, and then spend the rest of the night rearranging their furniture and dressing up in their clothes until they get back. So it did make me feel a bit better.

Until she told me who I was baby-sitting for.

Then it made me feel worse.

Much much much much worse . . .

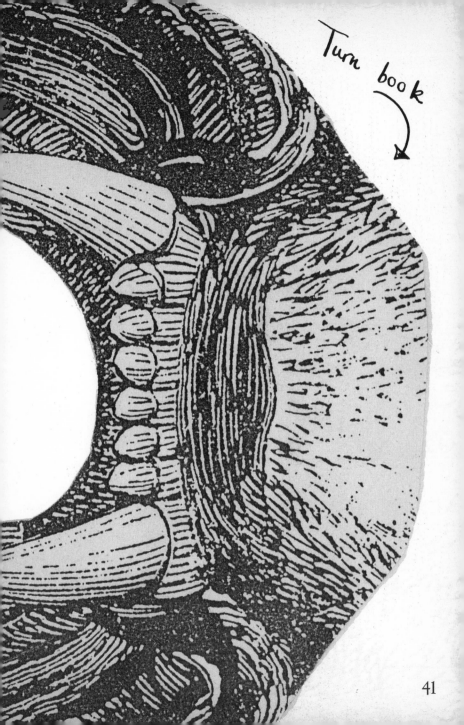

Turn book

41

Chapter Four

A friend will suffer if you don't pay attention

It was Geri.

I was being forced to baby-sit for Charlie's sister (or the Tasmanian Devil as I call her, which gives you some idea of what she's like).

And that wasn't all.

It wasn't a real baby-sitting job. Oh, no. Not in the accepted "get paid to go round to someone's house, eat all the cookies, and rearrange the furniture" sense.

No.

What I had to do was take Geri out and stand in a muddy field all morning watching Charlie play FOOTBALL.

Can you believe it?

What happened was this:

Apparently, Charlie's mum had promised to go
and watch him play, because it was a really
important game, he was really excited, bler
de bler de bler. . . .

Well.

We all know what happens
when mums promise to do
something, don't we?

Something else Comes Up.

And that's what had
happened.

Something
had Come Up,
which meant that Deirdre
couldn't go and

watch Charlie after all AND that she had no one to look after Geri. So she thought (in that oh-so-clever way mums have) that she'd kill two birds with one stone and get ME to take Geri to the match. (That is such a weird saying, isn't it? It'd be really hard to kill ONE bird with a stone, let alone two. And why would you want to, anyway? I don't know about you, but if I saw somebody trying to kill ANY birds with a stone, I'd go to the SPCA straight-away.)

Where was I?

Oh, yes. I tried to tell Mum that me going was hardly going to make Charlie feel any better, was it, and anyway I was FAR too upset about Dad to go out anywhere, but she wasn't having it.

It didn't look like I had any choice.

I was going to spend my Saturday morning standing in a muddy field with the four-year-old beast whether I liked it or not.

44

And that was that.

Deirdre was definitely plotting something. For the last couple of days her and Janet's mum had spent most of their time huddled over the kitchen table, giggling and whispering to each other, drinking enough coffee to sink a submarine. Every time I came in, they just smiled at me in that stupid "there's a good little boy, get along and play with your train set while us adults talk about important things" kind of way. And surprise, surprise, along came the day of the match and some crucial shopping had come up. The pair of them were off on some absolutely essential trip to buy eggcups or something. It makes you want to spit.

So I started the day of the big game feeling like I was already one–zero down. Then Deirdre told me Geri would be coming along to watch. Two–zero. But Janet would be there to cheer me on and keep an eye on the Thing That Bites, which perked me up and should have made the score even, except that Janet was in a really funny mood on the way to the field. I thought she was probably worried about her hair. It didn't look very princessy. It looked more like some huge bird had taken half of it away to make a nest.

I told her not to worry because it would grow back soon enough, and even if it didn't, there was nothing special about being a princess. Who'd want to marry the kind of idiot who thinks all sports have to be played on horseback, anyway?

She didn't even answer. Just looked off into the distance as though I wasn't there. Luckily, Johnny Ho joined us at that moment, so I didn't have to play that really annoying game of asking what's the matter to someone who isn't going to tell you but who's going to get mad if you don't ask.

Johnny and me spent the rest of the walk discussing tactics. He's good at that and didn't even mind that Geri spent most of the journey trying to bite his leg. I told her to stop it, but he said it didn't bother him, pain is only in the mind. His mind must have been hurting a lot in that case cos he kept making little *eek!* noises and wiping his eyes.

The sun was shining. The birds were singing. The Tasmanian Devil was sitting in the mud poking worms with a stick and muttering to

itself. I'd gotten myself something to drink from the snack bar.

And I still felt terrible.

All I could think about was my dad and how I'd never see him again. He was probably with that Beebee woman right now, pushing back a strand of hair from her face and smiling into her eyes with that special smile that just belongs to ME. . . .

Oh, I can't describe it. Just the thought of them together made the whole bright blue sparkly morning with the boys running round in their little white shorts and the dads shouting from the sidelines and the people walking their dogs look . . . gray.

Gray gray gray gray gray.

Like one of those old programs you get on TV sometimes that were made when my gran was little, before they were allowed to do them in color (maybe the world WAS black and white in those days. No wonder Gran's such a miserable old bat).

Where was I?

sad

Oh, yes, feeling really really sad.

I was SO sad, in fact, that I didn't even notice this big hairy dog that had come sniffing around. Not properly, anyway. And I usually ALWAYS notice dogs (they notice me too — probably because I might have been a dog in a previous life).

And then . . .

It was a bloodbath. By the time we got to the last ten minutes the score was still only three–two (to them — boo!!), and loads of time had been wasted with Ms. Lawrence, the home economics teacher, coming on to dress wounds or slap unconscious players round the cheeks (well, she did that to Mr. Kobek, the chemistry teacher, after he'd tripped over a stray dog and knocked himself silly for a moment, but then she has been a bit funny with him ever since they shared a pantomime horse in the local parade).

Still, a few knocks and bruises weren't going to stop my team going for it, and with the clock ticking down to the final minute, who should find himself clear on goal with only the hideous McTavish to beat? You guessed it. My chance for glory. Stick it in the net and earn the boys a great tie.

McTavish stood, huge and threatening, dead center in the goal area. There was only one way round him. Wait to the last minute, when he was committed to diving at the ball, then dodge sideways and around his grabbing hands. I watched his every tiny move as I thundered toward him. . . .

GERI!!!!!!!!!!!!!

She was gone.

GERI!!!!!!!!!!!!!

One minute she was there, playing this growly
game with the dog, and the next she was just —
gone. I shouted, I searched, I made the funny
whoop whoop whoop sound that always makes
her laugh. But it was no good. It was as if she'd
vanished off the face of the earth. . . .

Before

After

McTavish dived. I twisted round him and kicked the
ball, then I heard the shout and, for one critical
moment, I looked away. McTavish just got his hands
on the ball, knocked me flying, and landed on top of
me with a crunch. I was lying winded under a hundred

and twenty kilos of fat, sweaty French teacher, and my leg was twisted right up under me. The ball sailed over the net. Game over. We lost.

My leg hurt.

Well.

Charlie was absolutely furious. Apparently he'd slipped in the mud when he heard me shout for Geri, which made him miss the ball and hurt his leg a little bit. And THAT meant they lost the game and Charlie would most probably get dropped from the team forever and ever and never have another chance to play football again for the rest of his life.

Which, of course, was all MY fault.

Just because I was trying to find HIS sister.

How unfair is that?

So I started to get furious back. I told him that I'd never wanted to come and watch his stupid football match OR look after his stupid sister (who my mum says is ABSOLUTELY the worst-behaved four-year-old she's ever come across and although she likes Deirdre very much she can't imagine how she lets that child get away with what she does) and that I'd only agreed to do it because I felt SORRY for him. Then I said I knew all about how his mum had broken her promise to be there because something had Come Up. Which, I said, was probably that she found the prospect of watching a load of silly boys running around in mud about as thrilling as I did.

That shut him up.

So I left him standing there on one leg and went off home.

Some baby-sitter. It's just me, me, me with Janet sometimes and it's not exactly difficult keeping an eye on a four-year-old. Even with just one leg working properly it only took me seconds to find Geri. She was round the back of the snack bar rummaging through the bins with the dog that had tripped up Mr. Kobek. Any sensible person would have looked there first. I grabbed her under my arm and set off home.

Then something really horrible happened. I'd only
taken a couple of hops/steps when I felt all cold and
everything went swimmy. I sat down in the mud with a
bump and was really, really sick.

When I got in, Mum had that sparkly "I know
something you don't" look in her eyes. You
know the one. When they've got some really
exciting news but they're not just going to tell
you, they want you to weasel it out of them?
Well, I wasn't going for it. I was so fed up with
my life and angry with Charlie (and, even
though it wasn't my fault AT ALL, a bit worried
about Geri, actually) that I went straight to
my room to e-mail Tiff. That always makes me
feel better.

Well.

Whatever Mum had to tell
me obviously couldn't
wait, because she followed
me. She sat down on the
bed looking as if she was
about to explode. And then
she just came out with it.

She told me the news.

I must have passed out, cos the next thing I know, I'm lying on this table thing in a hospital with one football boot on and the other off. I could still taste the sick in my mouth, and I didn't feel much better when I looked at my ankle, which was blue and purple and orange and hurting a lot now.

I knew it was a hospital not just because there were screens round me and nobody to ask what was going on but because somebody suddenly screamed with pain, which made me feel a bit nervous. Then the screens opened, and in came a harassed-looking nurse with a tray of bandages. She explained that I'd sprained my ankle badly and that she was there to bandage it up.

As she started working on me, I heard an evil chuckle, then another nurse pushed the screens back and I saw a sight that cheered me up no end. A red-faced and tight-mouthed doctor limped in to look at my foot, and in the background there was Johnny trying to control a struggling Geri. There were bits of material in her mouth that exactly matched the doctor's trousers. That was when I realized it hadn't been a patient screaming earlier. It had been the doctor.

The doctor took one look at the bruises and told me I was very lucky I hadn't broken it. Whew! That was a near one! Then my whole world fell apart.

"Of course, you'll have to use crutches for a while."

Crutches???? Crutches?!!!! How can you snowboard on crutches?

"But not for a week or so." Another near miss! It seemed odd that I didn't need them now but would need them later, but I wasn't going to argue. Not when it meant I could still hit the snow.

From the end of the ward a worried voice called "Oh, Charlie!" and then there was Deirdre hurrying toward me. She looked really upset, but that wasn't the first thing I noticed.

The first thing I noticed was that she was pushing a wheelchair.

To: Tiffani
From: Janet
Subject: NEWS!!!!!!

Dear Tiff

You'll never guess what.

I'm going to France.

It's true.

I, Roxy Quicksilver, Board Babe Extraordinaire
and Queen of the Slopes (aka yr old mate), am
going to spend my Easter holiday in a house in
the French Alps (well, I say house. Apparently it's
more of a castle actually with about fifty-nine
bedrooms) with my mum and my sister and my
friend Charlie (we're going SNOWBOARDING! How
cool is that?) and his family. We shall be crossing
the English Channel (by boat, I suspect) and
driving down through the beautiful French
Countryside, stopping off, sans doute (that means
"without doubt"), to buy a chocolate croissant or
two at a picturesque café along the way (they use
the same word as us for café! How weird is that?
I bet we thought of it first).

This was set in Austria not France, you saddo! Dee

I AM GOING TO FRANCE!!!!!!!

And it is going to be SO cool. . . .

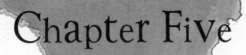

Chapter Five

A change of scenery will bring the unexpected

Well.

He'd only got a wheelchair, hadn't he.

CHARLIE had got himself a WHEELCHAIR!

Just because he'd slipped in the mud and hurt his ankle a tiny little bit.

I was SO jealous.

(I know it wouldn't be fun to be in a wheel-chair ALL the time, but just for a little while ... well, you must admit it WOULD be quite a laugh.)

The first thing I did was ask if I could have a go in it, of course. But he was really really grumpy and said no I could not, he needed it to get around believe it or not, because he actually had one of the worst sprains the doctor had ever seen and whose fault was that?

I chose to ignore him after that. I mean, you'd think he'd have got over his little accident by now (it was TWO DAYS ago, for goodness' sake!), but no. He spent the entire journey down through France (which took AGES — I had no idea France was so HUGE!!!!!!!) moaning on about how there wasn't any point in going anymore because he wasn't going to be able to go snowboarding!

As if the whole holiday was for HIS benefit!
Just because his mum had spent her entire life
savings on this really cool secondhand snowboard that he wasn't ever going to be able to
use! (That was what she and my mum went
out to get when she was supposed to be
watching him play football.)

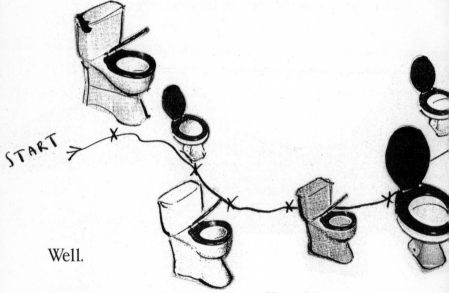

START

Well.

I tried to cheer him up by telling him not to
worry — the snowboard wouldn't go to waste
because I'D be able to use it. But that
just seemed to make him worse.

People can be so selfish, can't they?

Anyway.

What with Charlie moaning on about his
injuries, Mum getting an upset tummy (which
meant we had to do LOADS of extra stops in
all sorts of amazing places. My mum must
have gone to the toilet in virtually every town
in France. She could write a book about it:
Toilets in France: A Mother's Guide)
and Geri biting

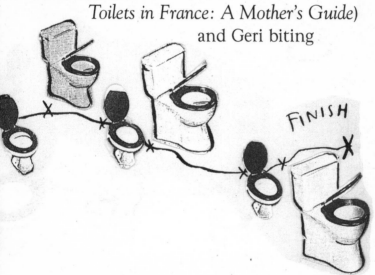

French people every time we stopped
(she reckons they taste better than English
people. It must be all the fine food they eat),
the journey just flew past.

And then we broke down.

This journey seemed to go on forever. I was stuck in my chair having to listen to Deirdre practicing her "Avay vooz" with Janet's mum at one end of Pegasus, while Dee (who refused to sit with the rest of us and had put up a dividing curtain at the back end) answered hundreds of calls from lovesick boys and dippy mates from back home. Meanwhile, Janet was being all overexcited about *everything*, even stupid stuff, like having hot chocolate for breakfast.

And I was really really BORED. All I could do was sit and look out the window, or sleep. It's vile being in a wheelchair, and don't let anyone tell you different. It looked like I was in for two weeks of hell.

It wasn't as bad as it sounds actually because we were NEARLY NEARLY there. The countryside had been getting more and more up and down the farther we went, and now it was REALLY hilly. Mountainous, in fact. I'd been a bit disappointed when we first got off the boat because everything looked quite like England (except for the signs being in French, of course), i.e., boring and flat, but this was different. I'd never seen mountains before, not in real life, and I was actually

quite amazed. They were so big and spiky and dangerous-looking. I couldn't wait to get up 'em.

Anyway.

COOL

We'd arrived in this village (or *"village"* as they call them in France!) and Deirdre suddenly went, "Oh, my goodness, this is it!" The house we were staying in was only about a mile away, just outside the village, halfway up the mountain!

So we all got really excited. Dee put her magazine away, and Charlie stopped moaning about his leg. Even Geri stopped work on the escape hole she was biting through the side of the bus.

And that was when it happened. Deirdre swung a left into this side street; the bus stalled and wouldn't start again.

We were stuck.

This was more like it! I almost fell out of my wheelchair from laughing. It was as though a dirty great whale had dropped out of the sky right into the middle of this little village and caused total havoc. The street was so tiny, Pegasus blocked it completely, and in no time at all we were the center of a sea of furious drivers, all waving their fists or trying to squeeze past. Then, best of all, a French policeman turned up. He obviously didn't have the vaguest idea what to do. Just stood there blowing his whistle, waving his arms around, taking abuse from everyone, and generally making things worse. It was great!

I was so embarrassed.....

I wouldn't have cared if we'd been in England. It was being Abroad that made it so bad. Think about it, we were probably the first English people they'd ever had in that village. And now they'd think we were all complete and utter der-brains who drive round in stupid hippie buses that break down in really awkward places, completely blocking the road so French people can't get home for their dinner.

I felt so embarrassed that when Geri said she needed to go to the toilet, I volunteered to take her. I thought we could disappear up a quiet alleyway away from all those honking cars and hide out until Deirdre managed to start the bus again. But then Geri said it wasn't the kind of toilet you could do up a quiet alleyway and Dee started saying this was the worst holiday of her life and why hadn't Mum let her stay at home on her own and the French people were still honking their horns and Mum shouted SHUT UP!

Well.

Once she'd got everyone's attention, Mum suggested that Deirdre and me take Geri to the place we were staying while she, Charlie, and Dee stayed with the bus and tried to get some help.

Well, I was all for that, so Deirdre drew Mum a map of how to get to the house once the bus was fixed, and off we went.

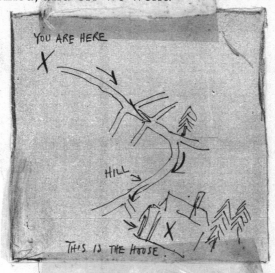

It took a while, but eventually the cop managed to unravel the mess a bit. Then, when Janet's mum had explained in her broken French that Pegasus refused to start, he persuaded a bunch of young guys who'd been enjoying the show from a nearby café to push the bus back round the corner, and the traffic began to flow again. Still, it couldn't stay there, so then he arranged for a truck to come and tow Pegasus off to a local garage, and we sat down to wait. I wondered how Janet was getting on.

It was getting dark by the time we arrived. Deirdre opened the door (it went *creeeeeeaaaak*,

just like a door in a horror film) and rushed
Geri inside to find the bathroom. So I was left
all alone to look round.

It was a bit scary actually.

Not because it WAS like something out
of a horror film (though it was quite old
and dusty-looking), but because it felt like
somebody had been there only a second ago.
Deirdre had told us it belonged to this old
friend of hers who used it for a couple of
months in the summer but left it empty all
the rest of the year because she couldn't stand
all the skiing holiday people. The thing was, it
didn't FEEL empty. There were ashes in the
fireplace and a pair of old boots on the rug,
looking as if someone had just that minute
kicked them off. There was a newspaper
spread out on the floor and a vase of daffodils
on the mantelpiece. Then I went through to
the kitchen and things started to get REALLY
weird.

We were still waiting for the truck to come when Dee,
who'd been sulking for the whole journey, suddenly
perked up (I could tell because the gloss had come
out again) and asked her mum if she could go and get
a cup of coffee. She hardly waited for an answer
before she was out of Pegasus and in there among

the bus-pushers, chatting and laughing as though she was a local. This was very strange because as far as any of us knew, she didn't speak any French.

Do you know the story of the *Marie Celeste*? It's about this big ship that was found years and years ago just drifting in the middle of the ocean. So these people that found it (whoever they were) got on board and had a look around.

Well.

Everywhere they went there were signs that people were there. Half-eaten meals on the tables (STILL HOT), half-drunk drinks in the bar. Cigars still smoking in the ashtrays. Saucepans still bubbling on the stoves. (Probably even an unflushed toilet in the bathroom!) But there was NO ONE THERE. Not a single solitary soul. It was as if everybody on that ship had just — disappeared.

And do you know what?

Nobody has ever found out what happened to those people.

How weird is that?

Anyway, that was EXACTLY what it was like in that kitchen in France (except for the bit about it being a ship. And the unflushed toilet, of course). There were dirty dishes piled up in the sink, and on the table was a mug and a coffee-pot and a plate with a half-eaten bit of bread next to an open book that looked as if some-body had been reading it just a second before.

I couldn't believe it. I just stood there. And stared.

Then I told myself that it actually wasn't weird at all — whoever lived here had probably just left in a bit of a hurry without clearing up (which would make sense if it was a friend of Deirdre's) and that if I touched the coffeepot it would definitely be completely and utterly stone-cold.

So I touched it.

And guess what?

It wasn't cold at all.

It was hot.

Finally, the tow truck arrived. It was huge, with a big
metal hook on the back. After a brief chat with the
driver, Janet's mum got back in and told me passengers
weren't allowed while the bus was being towed. She
said she'd leave me with Dee while she went to the
garage, then she'd come back for us in a taxi.

So that's what she did. I ended up sitting in my
wheelchair at the café, watching Dee flutter her eyelashes and giggle at her new friends, while Pegasus
disappeared sadly up the road.

I soon found out why Dee had hooked onto the bus-
pushing guys so easily. They weren't French at all.
They were a bunch of Brits. Cool snowboarding
dudes, just like me. Was I down with that. It was great
just hanging with them, giving it the verbals — almost
as good as really slipping the snow. Wicked!

My stomach did that horrible lurchy thing and the room started to whirl around me. All I could hear was this whooshing sound in my ears and the pounding of my heart. I tried to shout for Deirdre but it was like trying to shout in a dream — I opened my mouth and —

And then I realized I wasn't alone.

There was a man in the room. He was standing in the doorway, looking at me with a slight smile on his face.

And he was holding a knife.

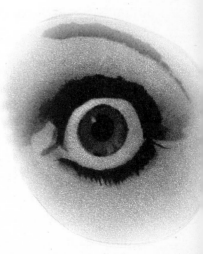

Chapter Six

People around you will behave strangely

It was only a butter knife, of course, but I was still pretty scared. I just stood there, staring, as if I'd seen a ghost. Then I thought maybe that was exactly what HAD happened (you know how your mind slows up when you're scared and you start thinking all sorts of weird things?) — maybe he really WAS a ghost. He looked a bit like one, standing there in the half-light, staring at me with these piercing black eyes (you know, the kind that look like they can see right through you and out the other side? A bit like Charlie's actually).

Anyway.

We seemed to stand there for ages, just staring at each other. All I could hear was the tap dripping in the sink and my heart beating in my ears.

And then he said it, quite calm and casual:

"Bonsoir."

He said *"BONSOIR"*!!!!!!! (Good evening 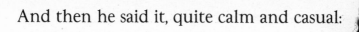 in French.)

And he said it in this really ordinary voice, just as if I was some old friend who'd wandered in off the street for a chat!

Then he said something else in French that I couldn't understand (let alone write down!) but I THINK meant something like who the heck (though he probably said some really bad French swear word instead of heck) are you and what d'you think you're doing in my kitchen? (He could have been admiring my hair, of course. I bet he'd never seen anything like THAT in France!)

Well.

I couldn't think of anything to say. Plus I couldn't speak French, of course. And there was no point making the situation any more

weird and complicated than it was already. So I
just said:

"I'm Janet."

For some reason this made him smile. He
raised one eyebrow and then repeated my
name as if he was testing it out:

"Ja-net."

Then he came right into the room, put the
knife down on the table (I'd already worked out
that he must've heard the others upstairs while
he was eating and gone out to investigate),
looked at me again with his bright black eyes,
and said (in English, thank goodness!):

"And you're from England, are you,
Mademoiselle Ja-net?"

Well.

This was such a silly question that I forgot all
about being scared.

"Of course I'm from England!" I said (I mean, how many French girls do YOU know called Janet?). "Where d'you think I'm from? Mars?!"

He stopped and pretended to think about that for a second.

"You could be from Mars," he said eventually. "We have no evidence that the red planet ISN'T entirely populated by small English girls called Janet. Except then," he continued, "it would not be called Mars at all. It would have to be called Planet Janet."

That was when I decided he couldn't be a ghost. I mean, I've heard a lot of ghost stories in my time and none of them has ever mentioned ghosts cracking jokes (even rotten ones like that). They're usually far too busy wailing and feeling sorry for themselves in drafty castles to see the funny side of anything. So I relaxed a bit and told him that I was staying here on holiday with my mum and —

And that was when Deirdre walked in.

I was getting on with the guys something fierce,
swapping stories about half pipes and slaloms and all
that stuff. OK, so I hadn't actually done any snowboarding for real, but how were they to know that? I'd
read the mags, which is more or less the same, and,
well, it would have been really uncool just to say that I
was on holiday with my mum and her friend and her
friend's daughter and our sisters, wouldn't it? Dee
wasn't listening, she was too busy playing Little Miss
Dude Magnet, so I knew she wouldn't drop me in it. I
could tell they were all really impressed because the
coolest guy of them all, Caleb, who had white hair in
the biggest spikes ever and a tattoo of a giant squid
wrapped round his neck, turned away from watching
Dee gloss her lips for a moment and gave me this
look. You know, the "you are one cool dude" look.

They just stared at each other. Just as if they'd
BOTH seen ghosts (but then if two ghosts met,
I don't suppose they'd be scared. Or surprised,
even. They'd just think, oh, hello, there's a
ghost like me, wonder if he's up for a bit of a
haunt).

Then the Frenchman swallowed and said:
"Deirdre?"

As if he couldn't believe it was really her.

"Deirdre?!"

Well.

You should've seen Deirdre's face. She went all
white. Then she went red. Then she went
white again with red blotches. She opened her
mouth to speak but the only sound
that came out was this funny little
squeaking noise, like a mouse with
    its tail caught in a trap.

EEK!!!

It was just as well Geri was there because it
was starting to feel like we could be there all
night. She was obviously just as fed up with all
this weirdo staring as me, so she dealt with it
in her usual way by creeping up on the French
bloke and sinking her teeth into his leg.

Well.

You would've thought that would get things moving along a bit, but while he was yelling and hopping round the room, Deirdre just grabbed Geri and legged it, leaving the two of us alone again together.

How bizarre was THAT?!

Things started going wrong when I told them I'd sprained my ankle landing after a triple overhead twist I'd been practicing. They all just stared at me for a moment, and the only sound was the smacking of Dee's lips as she glossed up for about the millionth time.

"A triple overhead twist, eh, kid?" Caleb asked, chewing slowly on a toothpick. "That sure is some jump."

I think I got a bit excited then, now they were all looking at me, dead impressed. Dee made a little humphing noise, like she didn't like me getting all the attention for once, but the guys kept on grinning and looking at me. They looked so interested, I got a tiny bit carried away.

"Yeah," I said, trying to look really cool, "I do them all the time. Quadruples too."

They all nodded admiringly at me, as Dee started scrabbling in her bag for a fresh lip gloss and making noises like her oxygen supply had been cut off. Caleb turned toward her.

"Quite a little whizzer, your brother," he said.

Dee frowned in the way only Dee can frown.

"Oo, yech! He's not my brother! He's got nothing to do with me. Just some scratty kid who hangs around all the time."

As soon as he stopped hopping and yelling I asked him what was going on. Did he and Deirdre know each other or something?

He didn't reply at first. And when he did he had this really funny look about him.

"We did," he said, staring into the middle distance in that annoying way grown-ups have when you know they've got a picture of something inside their head that they're not going to tell you about.

"Once upon a time we knew each other very well indeed."

Then he sort of shook himself and smiled.

"But that was a long long time ago. Over thirteen years, in fact."

Then he stopped. He looked at me and it was like he'd been turned to stone. I think he even stopped breathing.

Then he asked me how old I was. Like it was the most important question in the world.

Like his entire life depended
on the answer. So I told him.

And do you know what he
did?

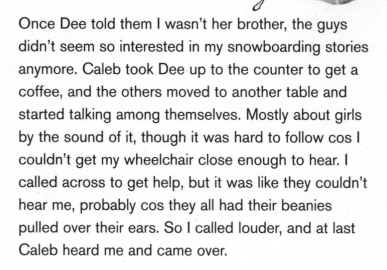

He started to cry.

Once Dee told them I wasn't her brother, the guys
didn't seem so interested in my snowboarding stories
anymore. Caleb took Dee up to the counter to get a
coffee, and the others moved to another table and
started talking among themselves. Mostly about girls
by the sound of it, though it was hard to follow cos I
couldn't get my wheelchair close enough to hear. I
called across to get help, but it was like they couldn't
hear me, probably cos they all had their beanies
pulled over their ears. So I called louder, and at last
Caleb heard me and came over.

Only, he didn't move me closer. He pushed me across
to the other side of the road. I asked him where we
were going. He said, "There's no WE, loser. And
there's no such thing as a triple overhead twist," and
he stamped off back to Dee and his mates, leaving me
stranded on the opposite sidewalk alone.

I wanted to kill the lot of them, but there was no way I could get back through the busy traffic without help. I just had to sit there grinding my teeth in frustration.

I reckon French people don't get so embarrassed about things as us, because he didn't seem to mind about the crying stuff (just like Deirdre! Perhaps that was why they'd got on so well). He blew his nose really quickly and told me his name was Paul (or "Poll" as they say in French). Then he told me about how he and Deirdre met on another holiday years ago in THIS VERY HOUSE and had got very "close" in a very short time (I reckon that means they were girlfriend and boyfriend!!!!! Ew!!!!! And he's well ancient!!!!!). At the end of the holiday they'd gone their separate ways and lost touch. Until today, of course. Paul reckoned the woman who owned the house must have forgotten that she'd told them BOTH they could use it for a holiday, which was why we'd all turned up at the same time (or maybe she did it on purpose, to try and get them back together?! That's what I reckon!).

Anyway.

Paul said it WAS a bit of a shock to see Deirdre after all these years (too right! Bet she didn't have purple hair and a nose ring when he last saw her!) but he was sure they'd sort it out later and not to worry because everything would be absolutely fine.

And before I had a chance to wonder why he thought I might be worried, he said something really amazing.

He said he was really glad it had happened because he'd met ME!!!!!

Well.

I thought that was pretty cool, but then he said something that was even cooler.

He suddenly jumped up from his chair and said he just had to have a picture of me!

Can you believe it?

Nobody had ever wanted a picture of me before (except Mum, of course. And all she's

Here I am!

got is one teensy little snap of me when I was a baby that she keeps in her wallet, which doesn't really count). Until now.

Paul wanted a PICTURE of ME!!!!!!!!!

I couldn't wait to tell Charlie.

Eventually Janet's mum turned up in a taxi. I can't tell you how glad I was to get away from those evil snow-sucking guys.

If it wasn't for my ankle, I'd have been pretty excited when I saw where we were staying. It was a huge old rambly place with ivy growing all over it and lots of turrets and stuff that would be great for exploring. Only I knew how I'd be spending my fortnight. I wouldn't be exploring. Oh, no. I'd be stuck on the ground floor, looking out the window, wishing I was back home.

Charlie Wells, this is your life. And it stinks.

I'd thought at first that Paul meant he wanted a PHOTO of me. But then he took me out the back of the house through the garden (which was more like a snow-covered JUNGLE actually and really hard to get through in the dark) into this big sort of outhouse building that was all full of paints and canvases and brushes and stuff. And it turned out he was an ARTIST and he wanted to paint my PORTRAIT.

A real live artist wanted to my paint my portrait!

Well. *happy*

You can imagine how I felt about THAT!

He said he wanted to start straightaway so he could capture the feeling he had in his heart when he first met me (French people are so poetic, aren't they? Maybe it's just cos they can't speak English very well), so I sat down on this dirty old paint-splattered chair and he got to work. I tried to keep as still as possible but it was pretty difficult. I just couldn't believe it was really happening. I was so happy I had to concentrate really really hard to stop myself from bursting out laughing because everything was so unbelievably fantastic! (I wonder if that's what was going on when that Mona Lisa woman was having her portrait done by Leonardo di Caprio? She always looks to me like she's trying not to laugh.)

And then Charlie arrived.

And that spoiled everything.

Chapter Seven

A new understanding will melt away like the snow

I'm not saying that what happened next was Charlie's FAULT or anything. I'm just saying that if Mum hadn't wheeled him into the room at that precise moment, then none of it would have happened.

Think about it. There I am, having my portrait painted by a genuine French artist, when in they come, without even knocking!

You would've thought Paul would ask them what the (bad French swear word!) they were doing, interrupting the progress of what could well turn out to be the greatest work of his entire career. But he didn't. He just put his brush down and looked at them, waiting for one of them to speak.

Well.

Nobody said anything for what seemed like ages. Then Mum made this sort of gulping noise in her throat and said:

"You must be Paul. We've been looking for you."

Der!

Grown-ups can say the most dopeyist of things sometimes, can't they? Especially when they're your parents.

Paul obviously thought it was a pretty dopey thing to say too, because he didn't reply. He just sort of nodded his head as if to say: "So what if I am, der-brain? What's it to you? I'm trying to get on with what might be the greatest painting of my entire career here, thank you very much!" But instead of taking the hint and leaving us to it, Mum said:

"Deirdre told me all about you."

Well.

For some reason that made Paul smile. He raised one eyebrow and sort of twinkled at her. Then he said:

"Indeed? I do hope she didn't tell you EVERYTHING about me."

He said it in this ha-ha-ha kind of way that quite frankly made me want to lose my lunch. I could tell Charlie was just as embarrassed as I was, but Mum didn't seem to mind. In fact, she went all sort of girly and giggly as if he'd just said the funniest thing in the world. Then she looked at him from underneath her eyelashes and started playing with the hair on the back of her neck. I decided I'd better put a stop to this before she did something TRULY grim, so I told Paul who she was.

"This is MY MUM," I said, thinking that would stop him waggling his eyebrows at her.

Well.

You'd think I'd said the most amazing and peculiar thing in the world. Paul did stop waggling his eyebrows. He stopped doing anything. He went all still again, like he'd been turned to stone. Then he turned to me.

"Your MUM?" he asked, as if he'd never heard of anyone having a mum before. "THIS is your mum, Janet?"

"Yeah," I said. I mean, who did he think she was — my grandma?! She's not THAT old! And then Mum went REALLY weird and said:

"And this is Charlie. Deirdre's boy."

Paul stared at me. Then he stared at Mum.

And then he stared at Charlie.

my mum, not!

Well, my vision of being trapped on the ground floor had come true sooner than I thought. The moment Janet's mum pushed me through the front door Deirdre leaped on her like a cat on a mouse and dragged her off upstairs somewhere, leaving me to watch Geri do her level best to swallow the hall carpet. I wondered what had got into Deirdre. She's pretty flaky at the best of times, but this time she looked like she'd been in a car crash or something.

Ten minutes later and Janet's mum came down on her own. I asked her what was up with Deirdre, but she only smiled and said it was nothing for me to bother about. Deirdre was just tired.

"Meanwhile," she said brightly, "there's someone we want you to meet."

Someone? What someone? Someone I was really going to get on with apparently, which made me deeply suspicious right off.

And I was right to be suspicious. After Janet's mum had wheeled me from one end of the house to the other, I finally found myself in a shed full of arty stuff, with two women talking gibberish to a French painter.

It was a dream come true. Almost as good as that one where I'm stuck in a pit full of snakes, and, just before they're all going to bite me, I find a trapdoor, dive through it, land headfirst in a chopper, and get made into burgers.

Could this holiday get any worse? Well, yes it could. I mean, it was bad enough them all talking nonsense to one other, but then this bloke starts grilling me too. Just like the burgers!

I couldn't believe it. One minute Paul was acting like meeting me had changed his entire life, the next it was as if I wasn't there at all. Like I was Mrs. Invisible or somebody! It was all Charlie Charlie Charlie. What was his name? How old was he? What had happened to his leg? Why had he come to France? Could he speak any French (as if!)? And (this one was REALLY weird) —

Hi! I'm Mrs. Invisible.

Was he any good at art?!!!!

Well.

When Charlie had told him who he was and how he'd come over with Deirdre and his sister and the rest of us, and no, he was rubbish at art but pretty good at football, Paul collapsed in a chair and hid his face in his hands. At first I thought he was crying again because his shoulders were all sort of shuddery. Mum must've thought the same because she kept looking at him with big wet eyes in this "oh the poor man I wish there was something I could do" way (you know the one) and chewing at her bottom lip.

But then he looked up and I realized we were wrong.

He wasn't crying. He was laughing.

And that was when I decided I'd had enough.

"Fine!" I said. "Great! Super! Wonderful!"

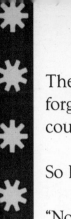

They all turned and looked at me as if they'd forgotten I was still there (which they had of course).

So I said:

"Now we've all established exactly who we all are and how incredibly amazing and hilarious everything is, perhaps you two could clear off and leave me and Paul to get on with our work? Yeah?"

Well.

You'd think that was a reasonable enough request, wouldn't you? But nobody moved. They just stayed there, looking at me. Mum opened her mouth as if she wanted to object, but I wasn't having that. I marched over to Charlie's wheelchair and started heaving it toward the door.

Mum said, "Janet," and Paul got up out of his chair. But I took no notice. I just kept pushing. All I wanted was to get Mr. Fascinating Wheelchair out of there, so Paul could get on with my portrait and everything could be like it was before they came in. Trouble was, the chair was more difficult to maneuver than I'd expected and I didn't notice this big can of red paint near the door until it was too late. Over it went, the paint glooping out all over the floor like blood or that red-hot stuff that comes out of volcanoes. It went everywhere, all over Charlie's wheels, all over my shoes — everywhere.

Mum said "JANET" again (like it was MY fault the paint had been left in such a stupid place!) and looked at Paul in this "what can you do, I'm just her mother, aren't kids awful?" kind of way she's got, which quite frankly irritates the pants off me. So I said:

"Fine" (again). "If you want to paint Wheelchair Boy's picture instead of mine, that's absolutely fine! Because I've actually got far better things to do with my time than hang around in here with a bunch of saddoes like you!"

Then I walked out.

Ha!

That showed them.

And then there were just the two of us because Janet's mum ran after her. I tried to give her the sad little look I'd been working on since I'd been in the wheelchair. The "I can't do anything on my own and I really need you to stay with me and look after me" look, but she didn't seem to notice. Actually, I was so desperate not to be left on my own with the creepy painter that I grabbed the back of her jacket as she was heading for the door, and she dragged me for a meter or two before she managed to shake me off.

Oh, wormholes! Stuck having to make polite conversation with Mr. Waggly Eyebrows.

I tried to disappear by pulling my head down inside my collar, but it just wouldn't go.

I pushed through the bushes at the side of the garden and found myself in this dark lane. I didn't know where I was going and I didn't care. I didn't care about anything (though I was starting to wish I'd gone to the toilet before I left).

It was SO UNFAIR. To have someone make out you're the greatest thing that's ever happened to them and then, like, *nothing* . . .

Anyway.

I'm quite scared of the dark when I'm indoors, alone in my bedroom, because you hear all these strange noises and you don't know what they are.

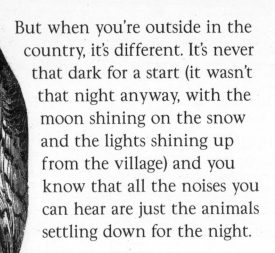

But when you're outside in the country, it's different. It's never that dark for a start (it wasn't that night anyway, with the moon shining on the snow and the lights shining up from the village) and you know that all the noises you can hear are just the animals settling down for the night.

Which makes you feel quite cozy. So when I realized that I'd walked quite a long way from the house, I wasn't worried. I was pretty COLD because I hadn't stopped to put on my coat, and I REALLY needed to go to the toilet by this time, but I wasn't worried. I reckoned I'd just keep on going until I reached the village.

Then I could find somewhere to go to the loo (well, I wasn't going to go outside, was I? Not in THAT weather!), have a bit of a look around at the shops, and then wander back to the house when I felt like it (by which time they'd all be wondering where I'd gone and feeling really really bad at the way they'd treated me).

Trouble is, when I reached the village there wasn't anywhere to go. Round where we live at home there are shops and stuff open all night, but not here, oh, no. Everything was all closed up and quiet. And I was getting REALLY cold. And I REALLY REALLY needed to go to the loo.

Sooo desperate...

And then I spotted it. The café near where the bus had broken down. The tables and chairs had all been moved inside but the lights were still on, so I reckoned it must be open.

So I went inside.

There was a long silence. I kept hoping he'd go away and leave me alone. If I could I'd have left on my own, I would have, but that's another one of the problems with a wheelchair. You can't make quick getaways. And you can't make getaways at all when there's paint all over your wheels, not without getting your hands covered.

I couldn't stand it any longer, I had to say something. But what did I know about painting, or being French? So I started to tell him what an interesting shed it was. Only, he began speaking at the same time, so we both stopped and then it was even more embarrassing. I looked all round, hoping that Deirdre would come in and rescue me, but there was no sign of anyone. Then he cleared his throat and asked me if I needed pushing anywhere.

Well, it was a pretty stupid question, considering it was obvious that I was desperate to get out of there, but you've got to be polite, haven't you? Especially when your ankle's sprained and you're totally dependent on a strange French bloke to help you out. Anyway, I asked him to push me back to the house cos I was worried about my sister and the hall carpet. He said fine, and started pushing me toward the door.

We'd only gone a couple of meters when he stopped. I twisted round in the chair and saw that I'd left big long red tracks on the floor, and he was looking at them.

"Very interesting," he said, "very interesting. Still, we can't take you into the house like that. The paint will ruin the floor." Just my luck, still stuck with him. But then he smiled and clapped his hands. "No problem!" he said, and the next thing I know, he's picked me up out of the chair and is striding up the garden with me in his arms like a baby. Aaaaarrrrrrrgh!

Well.

I was just wondering how to say, "Can I use your toilet, please? I'm desperate," in French, when I heard this voice behind me.

"Well, well, well," it said. "Look who's here! The weird-hair kid off the magic bus! Wonder what SHE'S doing out so late all on her own?"

I turned round to see this really cool-looking boy with an octopus tatooed on his neck. I was just about to tell him that it was none of

his business WHAT I was doing when he
smiled and stuck out his hand.

"Hi," he said. "I'm Caleb. Want a drink?"

Chapter Eight

You will feel that you are not getting enough attention

Well.

What would you do if some really cool boy asked you if you wanted a drink?

That's right. I wrote to tell my best friend all about it.

Hey Tiff!
It feels quite weird to be writing you a real letter. But guess where I am?? You know I told you I was going to France? Well I'm here! And I'm having the most FANTASTIC time! Charlie's being a pain (no change there, then!), Dee's puking her guts up because of some bug or other, and Mum's spending all her time drinking red wine and being mysterious in corners with Deirdre. But do you know what?

I DON'T CARE!

I've made friends with these really cool snowboarders down in the village. We've been hanging round

together for a few days now and guess what?
They're TEACHING ME TO SNOWBOARD!!!!

How cool is that? !!!!!!

I know what you're thinking, Tiff, but I am actually getting quite good! In fact the other day, Caleb (he's, like, the coolest one of the group and he's REALLY good-looking!) said he reckoned I had what it takes to become a pro!!!!!!!

What d'you think about that?! Me, professional snowboarder extraordinaire (i.e., extraordinary), known throughout the world for my death-defying stunts.

Which reminds me — if I AM going to be a professional snowboarder I'd better get out there and practice. The gang'll be waiting for me on the slopes!!!!!!

Wish me luck!

Love, your supercool snowboarding best friend

Janet

Roxy Quicksilver, Board Babe Extraordinaire and Queen of the Slopes, Passionflower Poisson

Luckily there was nobody around when Paul carried me back into the house, but all the same I felt like a complete jerk. He stuck me down in an armchair in this big old room off the hall, then just stood there looking at me for a minute while I fidgeted around wishing I was somewhere else. Then he caught hold of the arms of the chair.

"I have something very important to say to you, Charlie," he said. Oh, stinky cheese! My heart sank. Whatever next? Somebody help me, please!

He took a deep breath, then knelt and looked me straight in the eyes.

"When I carry you in my arms just now, I bet you feel — how do you say? A complete jerk!"

And that did it. I started laughing, then he started laughing, and he slapped me on the shoulder and did this silly little dance that was so stupid, I started laughing some more. Then he did an impression of Janet stamping out of the room followed by a funny face that I knew at once must have been my expression when I found myself all alone with him. He even looked a bit like me in a weird, French sort of way!

And that really made me howl. I laughed so much I thought I was going to turn inside out.

Well.

To be honest the holiday wasn't turning out to be QUITE as much fun as I'd told Tiff. I was rubbish at snowboarding and all Caleb wanted to talk about was DEE. Did she have a boyfriend back home? (Like she'd tell ME if she did!) Why didn't she ever come down to the café? Would I bring her with me next time I came?

I was beginning to wonder if it was me he was interested in at all!!!!!!

Anyway.

When I told him Dee was lying in bed in a sweaty old nightgown with her hair all tousled, moaning and groaning and ordering Mum to bring her drinks at regular intervals, I reckoned that would shut him up. It didn't though. If anything it seemed to get him even MORE interested — he said could he have her

cell-phone
number (like
she'd ever give it to
ME!!!) and told me to let
him know the minute she
was ready to see anyone.

How weird was that? BOYS!
I'LL NEVER
understand
them!

Boys, eh?

You know, he's all right, Paul. I thought he was going
to be some arty-farty sort of bloke, but actually, he's a
good laugh, AND he went off to get us some grub —
which was great because I was feeling pretty hungry
by then, as my whole family had totally forgotten that I
need to eat sometimes. I was a bit worried what he'd
bring me. I expected him to bring a load of weird
stinky French scoff, but — guess what? — he made
cheese on toast! I didn't know it was cheese on toast
until he told me, cos it was the wrong shape bread
and the wrong color cheese and the wrong taste, but
it was brilliant, the best cheese on toast ever!

Anyway, we ended up just sitting and chatting for
ages. He was pretty cool for a wrinkly and knew about

loads of stuff. He even knew about football. He'd actually been at the match when France won the World Cup against Brazil and described every shot and every pass in fascinating detail. He said that, as an artist, it was one of the most beautiful things he'd ever seen. But then he suddenly stood up and said I had to see his work. Shame. And we'd been getting on so well.

I tried to say I was tired, but Paul wasn't having any of it. He fetched the wheelchair (the paint had dried by now, so he could bring it through the house), I climbed into it, and he pushed me off back to the shed, singing happily to himself. On the way he kept stopping midsong and asking me really crazy questions. Do I dream in colors? Can I waggle my ears? Which do I prefer, roast potatoes or french fries? (Chips, I corrected him! But he took no notice.) I'd assumed we were going to the shed, but we followed the path round past it. The garden opened out into a much bigger space behind it, and guess what was there? A bigger shed! A much bigger one. In fact, I think you'd have to call it a barn. It was huge and black, like a giant spaceship blotting out the stars. Paul stopped and turned to me in the gloom, smiling.

"Now you'll see something," he said. "This is where I do my REAL work." And he shoved me through the barn door.

I was totally gobsmacked. The barn was huge, even bigger inside than it looked from the outside, and there were paintings on both the long walls. Not lots of paintings. Just two. One on each wall, but they were gigantic! Bigger than London buses! You'd need a ladder to get to the top of them and a bike to get from one end to the other (there was a paint-spattered bike propped up at one end of the barn — maybe that was what it was for). But the best thing about them was they were . . . erm, how shall I put it? WILD!!!!! Like somebody'd got loads and loads of tins of paint and just gone completely mad chucking them about! Brilliant! Just like having a food fight, only with paint, and no cleaning up or telling off! If this was art, I might have to change my mind about it.

"What do you think?" Paul said, and I had to tell him. That made him smile even more, and he asked if I wanted to see how they were done. Do you know what? I did! Me, Charlie Wells, superstar player and soon-to-be art enthusiast!

Dear Dad,
Having a great time here in the French Alps but miss you loads. Charlie's boring. Dee's sick, and Mum's ignoring me.
Wish you were here.
Love
Janet
x x x x x x x x x x x x

I tried to make friends with Charlie again the other day. I thought he must be getting a bit fed up, stuck around the house all day with no one to talk to (except Paul, of course, but he doesn't count cos Charlie HATES art), plus I was getting a TINY bit bored with snowboarding, so I offered to push him down to the village.

Well.

You'd think he'd be grateful, wouldn't you?

He wasn't, though. He looked at Paul and said
no thanks, him and Paul were a bit busy today.

And when I said what could you two possibly
be busy with, he just went "you'll see." Then
they smiled at each other in this stupid
secretive way as if they were the only two
people in the world that mattered.

Which quite frankly irritated the pants off me.

I mean, I'M the one who Paul was first
interested in. I'M the one he wanted to paint.
And I'M THE ONE WHO'S INTO ART. It was
all SO not fair that I decided to go down to the
village on my own.

I didn't need them.

I had Caleb and my snowboarding mates.

me

It was just like I thought. The paintings were done by
chucking stuff around! Some of the marks were even
tire tracks from where Paul'd ridden the bike all over
them. What a great idea! Though I told him I didn't
think it was what I'd call art. But he reckoned that the
REALLY important thing about art wasn't the picture
or the sculpture or whatever you ended up with, it
was the DOING IT IN THE FIRST PLACE. He said
anything could be art, even football, if you did it right.
It really didn't matter if whatever it was lasted forever
or just disappeared overnight. That got me thinking.

The next thing he said really threw me though. He
said that seeing the tracks my wheelchair had made in
the paint had given him an idea for a project, and I
was an essential part of it.

Well.

The gang wasn't at their usual table in the café, so I started off up the slopes to look for them. It was pretty cold that day (I think it'd been snowing in the night again) and I was actually feeling a bit fed up with it all. I mean, snow's all very well when you can build snowmen with it and throw snowballs and everything. But you can't do that with French snow for some reason. It's all dry and powdery and doesn't stick together properly like it does in England.

I remember one time at home (I must've been quite little because Dad was still living with us) when me and Dee woke up and looked out the window and the whole world was white (it must've been a REALLY long time ago actually because it was before Dee turned into the Lip-Gloss Monster. She actually used to speak to me in those days). Anyway, we all bundled up in scarves and gloves and stuff (even Mum didn't say she was too busy for once) and rushed out to the park and played in the snow for hours and hours and hours. . . .

But you can't do that with French snow. And when the world's white ALL the time it's not special. It's just white.

Paul's idea was brilliant, and we spent the next week planning it. Nobody else took any notice. Janet was off somewhere doing her own thing, and Deirdre seemed quite happy to have me spend my time with Paul. She and Janet's mum spent most of their time sitting in the kitchen, drinking wine and muttering together, and looking up and saying, "Were you looking for something, Charlie?" every time I wheeled in, in that way that means "push off and leave us alone." Dee was just a moaning noise from upstairs. And as for Geri — well, fresh bite marks appeared here and there every day, so she must have been around somewhere.

We had to take one day off from our planning because this reporter woman came from London for the day to take photos and talk to Paul. Apparently, he'd been quite famous once. I spent the time trying out my crutches and a pot of green paint in the barn. It's really easy, this art stuff, once you know what you're doing. I did "Picture of Mr. McTavish in Green Blobs" by Charlie Wells. When the reporter had packed up and gone, Paul took a look at it and said he thought it was pretty good for a beginner and that he sensed that I had strong feelings about the subject of the picture. Got that in one!

Anyway, finally everything was prepared and we were ready to create our great masterpiece. On the day, a fresh layer of snow had fallen. Perfect!

By the time I found Caleb and the gang up on the slopes it was getting REALLY cold. And Caleb didn't seem very pleased to see me. In fact, as soon as he saw that Dee wasn't with me he just took off on his board and disappeared. None of the others seemed particularly interested in talking to me either (they never are actually) so I just hung around for a bit watching and getting cold.

Eventually I got fed up. Caleb hadn't come back and I'd forgotten to bring Charlie's board so I couldn't go after him. And all the others were still ignoring me. So I went over and asked Caleb's best mate (his name's Simeon and he looks a bit like Charlie actually) if I could borrow his board to go off after Caleb.

Well.

You'd think I'd asked if I could borrow his underpants!

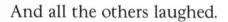

He looked at me as if I was completely and utterly raving mad and said, "Use MY board on THAT slope? No way! I don't want your blood all over it!"

And all the others laughed.

When I asked him what he was on about (I mean, I might not be the best board dude on the planet, but I'm not THAT bad), he said: "Listen, kid. That slope is just about the most difficult and dangerous round here — if an inexperienced little squirt like you tries to go down it you'll most likely end up DEAD."

Then one of the others said something about that wouldn't be much of a loss would it and they all laughed again and wandered off to talk to this group of French girls who'd turned up.

119

It was awful.

Then I noticed that one of the girls had left her board lying under a tree. So I picked it up. I was going to go and give it to her but when I looked over they were all laughing together and I didn't want to interrupt.

So I went over to the start of the slope.

How difficult could it be?

I took a deep breath and put the board down on the snow.

The slope didn't look THAT steep. . . .

120

Chapter Nine

Danger brings you closer to an important person in your life

The morning was cold and crisp and sunny and, as Paul and me made our way out to the big space behind the garden, I just knew that we were going to do something brilliant. You could smell it in the air.

It hadn't been so brilliant earlier, though, when Janet had appeared, wanting to know if I'd like to be pushed down to the village to meet all her new snowboarding friends.

I'd wondered what had brought on this "let's be friends" stuff all of a sudden. She'd been ignoring me ever since we'd arrived. It proved just how much attention she'd been paying me, cos I'd been mostly on crutches for the last couple of days. I was on them even while she was asking me. So I just hadn't been in the mood to join in with whatever girl game she was playing. I'd told her I was busy with something more important.

Well, that set her off. Her eyes went all squinty and she wanted to know what was so important about spending all my time with a really boring old bloke. So I said it was better than spending my time with a load of losers who thought that skidding around on the snow was the only thing worth living for, or worse still, a snotty little kid who just hung around with those losers. So she said . . .

Well, you know how it goes. She stomped off in a snit after calling me a lot of words I bet her mum doesn't know she knows, and I went back to filling my wheel-chair with all the stuff me and Paul had been gathering for our big creation. I was really glad to see the back of her. I mean, if Janet was a real friend, she wouldn't have left me on my own all week, would she?

Anyway, I soon forgot about her. Because Paul is just so enthusiastic about things it's really hard not to get enthusiastic too. Now we were out here in the lovely crisp snow, with him pushing my wheelchair full of goodies, and me hopping along behind, making interesting crunchy noises with my crutches.

It was the best feeling in the world.
Flying over the snow with the wind
in my hair and the cold making
my eyes water. I remember thinking,
how could Simeon say this
slope was DIFFICULT? It's the
easiest thing in the world! All
you have to do is just stand
on the board and let the
world whistle past your ears.

I understood for the first time
why people like snowboarding
so much (or skiing or
parachuting or hang gliding or
any of those things) — I mean I
always knew it was FUN, but it's
not just that. It's because it makes
you feel like nothing matters. All
the silly little problems, the
things that you seem to spend
all your days and most of your
nights worrying about —
being jealous of Charlie, my
dad getting married, feeling
left out by the snowboarding

gang — they just didn't seem to
matter anymore. Dad would
always love me whether he was
married or not. Charlie was still
my friend. And the gang? They just
weren't worth bothering with at all.
The things that really mattered
would always be there and the rest
of the stuff was like a flurry·of
snowflakes in the wind. There was
just me. And the mountain.

And it was great.

Paul's idea had been inspired by the paint marks left
by my wheelchair. He'd thought about what they'd
look like in the snow. The crutches too. He reckoned
they'd be like animal tracks, which tell a kind of story.
For instance, when you can see that a rabbit's been
chased by a fox, and they've run round a tree, then the
rabbit's disappeared into a bush and the fox has
walked off really fed up, or something like that. But
our story would be a MYSTERY.

Earlier in the week Paul'd shown me all these pictures
of crop circles, these really strange patterns that

appear in fields of wheat overnight. The story behind them was a mystery too. Nobody really knows where they come from, though some blokes with beards and thick glasses reckon they're done by flying saucers. (Other people reckon they're done by blokes with beards and thick glasses.) They're obviously bonkers. I'd have thought aliens had far better things to do with their time, like world domination or sucking brains. Anyway, we were going to do something similar (crop circles, not brain sucking), only it would be much, much more interesting. We were going to use my wheelchair and crutches to make weird patterns and then add funny-shaped bits of wood and splodges of color so it looked like SOMETHING really exciting had happened.

I usually hate being on my own. It makes me feel like I don't really exist — that I could just disappear at any second like a bubble — but this was different. I felt really really alone when I was flying down that mountain — like I was the only person in the entire universe — but I didn't feel lonely. I felt like I could do anything and be anything and that I didn't need anybody else because it was just so great being me. . . .

I felt happy, I suppose.

I just felt really really happy.

I thought building snowmen and having snowball fights was fun, but this was loads better. Paul picked out a huge flat area of snow with a tree smack in the middle as our "canvas" and we started.

We built four small pyramids out of lumps of old branches and bits of driftwood Paul had collected on his last holiday, and put them at the corners of a big diamond round the tree. Then Paul pushed me round and round each one in the wheelchair so we made lots of wiggly-waggly double-lined circles. After that we made a load of long straight lines with dotted lines between the circles (me on crutches dragging one foot in a ski), crisscrossing each other like a chess-board with spots. To finish those off we wrapped different bits of brightly colored cloth round some small rocks and put them in the holes the crutches had made so they looked like colored counters. To do this we reached over and dropped them from a little fishing net on a stick. That way there were no footprints. Whenever we did have to walk on the snow, we used a broom so we could wipe out our footprints as we went.

Soon an area about the size of a field was covered with the pattern of strange little brown-and-black wooden structures circled by tire tracks, and the chessboard with brightly colored counters. It looked brilliant, especially against the bright white snow, and as we'd got rid of all our footprints, it was really, really mysterious. You could imagine someone coming along and seeing it and trying to work out how it had got there. It would totally do their head in.

There was one last thing Paul reckoned we needed to do to finish it properly. Something big. So we tied the wheelchair to the tree with a long rope. The idea was to push it round and round in circles so that it made a great whirly pattern smack the middle as a kind of centerpiece for our design. We'd got it all set up and were about to get started when Paul realized he'd forgotten his camera, so he left me sitting in the wheelchair while he dashed back to the house. After all, we knew our work was going to disappear as soon as it snowed again, but it looked so good we had to get a picture of it.

While he was away I began thinking about Janet. Even though I was still a bit annoyed with her, I couldn't help thinking what a shame it was she was missing all this. ART was her thing, after all, and she'd have loved to've been a part of it. Of course, it was her own silly fault for being all moody and difficult, but I couldn't help thinking it would have been more fun with her around.

Still, I couldn't help that. If she wanted to hang around with a load of losers, that was her lookout. Meanwhile, I had something to be proud of. I looked all round, admiring MY work. Who'd have thought it? Charlie Wells, professional footballer AND famous artist.

I was already planning my next masterpiece when I heard the scream.

Have you ever been completely and utterly positive that you're going to die?

I have.

This is what happened.

I was whizzing down the slope, enjoying the ride and thinking happy thoughts about life in general, when I suddenly noticed that the slope was getting quite steep. Then it got very steep. And then it got so steep that it wasn't really a slope anymore. It was more like a sheer drop. A sheer drop that I was hurtling down on a snowboard I couldn't control.

Well.

I started going faster, of course.

That's what happens when you go down a very steep slope on a snowboard.

I went faster and faster and faster and I knew there was no way in the world I was ever going to be able to stop and all I could do was hope and pray that I'd land in a nice soft pile of snow and wouldn't break too many bones.

But it was not to be.

I looked down.

And that's when I realized it was all over.

There was a big space at the bottom of the hill. I could see it quite clearly laid out beneath me. And I remember thinking, How strange. It looks as if two giant children have been playing snakes and ladders in the snow.

It looked really amazing — all laid out like a board game, you see, with squares and lines and colored dots that looked like counters. And a little dark shape that could have been a person sitting on some kind of seat....

And right in the middle was this great big pine tree....

Well.

Have you ever been so scared that you're not really scared anymore? That's how I felt when I realized I was going to hit that tree.

Everything seemed to slow down and I found myself thinking incredibly clearly. My brain thought, Oh, dear, I do hope somebody will find me and tell Mum so she can arrange to have my body flown back to England so I can be given a decent burial. . . .

I was just thinking about my funeral and how sad everybody would be when I realized that I wasn't going to hit the tree at all. Everything speeded up again and came rushing toward me in a blur and I heard myself scream and all of a sudden I REALLY REALLY REALLY didn't want to die so I grabbed at this thing flying past my head and the next thing I knew I was whirling round and round and round and round and I realized that it was Charlie's wheelchair I was hanging on to and that Charlie was in it and he was yelling and shouting and then —

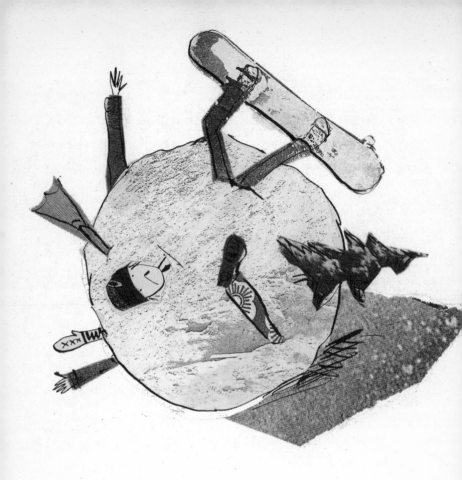

Everything stopped.

I wasn't dead after all.

I was lying in the snow with Charlie in a big tangle of legs and rope and wheelchair.

And we were laughing.

Typical, isn't it? One moment I'm thinking what a shame it is she's not there. The next, well, she couldn't be any closer. We're in a great heap, tied together, nose to nose, covered in snow and bits of wheelchair. I was only just beginning to clear my head and work out what had happened when I heard this howl of laughter. The next thing, a flash went off, and there's Paul with his camera, catching us stuck together like a right pair of idiots.

Now I know what people mean when they say they have to suffer for their art.

Chapter Ten

You will keep a very special secret

Do you know what the best thing is about going on holiday?

Coming home.

It is. Even if you've had a BRILLIANT TIME (which I had, of course), it's just so great to walk back through your own front door into your own house and smell its old familiar smell. It's a funny thing, but you don't realize your house smells when you're living in it, do you? I don't mean like a stinky horrible smell, I mean just a smell. Quite a nice smell usually — a combination of the soap your mum buys and the coffee she drinks and the stuff she squirts down the loo and then complains because somebody always uses it (the loo, I mean) before the stuff gets a chance to work. Then there's Dee's endless body spritzers and antistinky armpit sprays and polish and bleach and dust and that really nice electric smell you get off the TV and Mum's perfume and a tiny weeny whiff of Dad's leather jacket from the last time he visited.

Ooh, it was good to be home.

We'd had a brilliant second week in France. Janet forgot all about the stupid snowboarders, and her, Paul, and me spent our time painting and building and making all kinds of stuff. Soon half the mountain was covered with our pieces. It was just one big laugh from beginning to end. Though the biggest laugh came when we were leaving.

Deirdre finally got Pegasus back from the garage. It hadn't been hard to fix. It turned out to be a problem with the air filter. Apparently they're not supposed to have mouse nests in them. The mechanic dragged it out, charged her a small fortune, and the old bus was in top form again.

Saying good-bye was difficult, what with having to leave Paul behind and having to detach Geri from his leg. On top of which Deirdre was still being peculiar and would only give him a little wave from the bus. She just didn't seem to like him. No reason. Just being Deirdre.

Anyway, we finally got moving. Deirdre was driving even worse than she normally does. It didn't help that Janet's mum stayed right up close, whispering to her and patting her hand. We had a few near misses going down the hill, then took the wrong turn and ended up going back through the village. And who was sitting around outside the same café again? Hideous Caleb and his mates, all trying to look super-cool, with their snowboards propped up in a pile on the curb.

They didn't look cool for long though. Deirdre suddenly made this funny little choking noise, and the bus swerved and bounced onto the pavement. It was only a moment before she got it under control again, but it was just long enough to send the snowboarders scattering in panic and smash their snowboards to pieces. They came running after the bus, shouting and waving their fists in fury, but only Janet and me saw them. We waved back and smiled, then Janet turned to me with this pretend sad look on her face and we laughed ourselves sick.

But now it was good to be home.

What made it even better was that Paul had given us both presents before we left. Mine was sort of flat and square and Charlie's was round (no prizes for guessing what THAT was!) and we'd both promised not to open them until we got back.

Well.

You can imagine how difficult it was not to peek on the journey (why is it that the journey back is always so much longer than the journey there? I shall have to write a book about that one day) but I'd promised to wait so I did.

Anyway.

The minute we walked in the door Mum put
the kettle on, Dee rushed off to make sure that
none of her clothes had gone out of fashion
while we'd been away, and I ripped open
my parcel.

You'll never guess what it was.

No, you won't, so I'm going to tell you.

It was a painting.

Of me.

Paul had done a painting of ME!

It was the one he'd started when we arrived.
He must've finished it in secret and it was
absolutely BRILLIANT. It made me look — well,
not pretty exactly (it's quite hard to look pretty
when you've been painted with lopsided
green hair and mad-looking purple eyes) but
very very INTERESTING (you could tell it was
me in spite of the green hair and mad eyes
because Paul is such a BRILLIANT artist. And
because he'd written JANET in ginormous

orange letters across the top). You felt like I was going to do something any minute — you couldn't tell WHAT — I might laugh or cry or scream or yell or jump to my feet and disappear out of the painting — but I was definitely going to do SOMETHING. A bit like the Mona Lisa, I suppose. But not as brown.

Mum said I had to REALLY look after it because it might be worth a lot of money one day because Paul had started to get famous again recently. Apparently some woman from an English newspaper had come over to do an interview with him while we were there because everybody who was anybody in the Art World was talking about him having a comeback.

Well, I didn't care about any of that obviously.
I'm not going to look after my painting
because it might be worth a lot of money
one day.

I'm going to look after it because I love it.

And it's mine.

The very very best thing about coming home wasn't
home. It was me. Or to be exact, my ankle. I'd been
out of the wheelchair and on crutches for the last
week, hopping around without them now and again
as long as someone helped me. But now, after what
seemed like years, I could walk again on my own. It
was slow at first, as my ankle was still weak, but that
didn't stop me getting around. It felt great, even though
I looked like I was about four hundred years old.
Walking is the most brilliant thing in the whole universe.
You just don't know how good it is until you can't do it
anymore.

And this was my cue to open my present from Paul.
He'd said I could open it when I got back, but it would
be better if I waited until I was on my feet again. Well,
I'd waited, and now it was time.

To: Tiffani
From: Janet
Re: FAMOUS ME!

Hey Tiff, you'll NEVER guess what! The most
AMAZING thing has happened!

My picture is all over the Sunday papers! I know
it sounds unbelievable but it's true!

You know I told you about how me and Charlie
met this painter bloke in France?

Well. He did this portrait of me (apparently I was
the best model he's ever had!) which everybody
thought was SO good (probably because it makes
me look INCREDIBLY pretty, ha-ha) that they've
done this big write-up about him in the paper and
they put my portrait on the cover of the magazine!

How cool is that?!

Love
Your FAMOUS friend

Mona Lisa Venus de Milo Belladonna la
Serenissima Pesce (aka JANET)

144

Before I could open the present, a madly excited Janet came running in, waving this magazine around. Her portrait was only on the front cover. Paul had already showed me the painting, so that wasn't a big deal, but seeing it on the front of a national paper. Wow! That was really something.

She was in and out in a flash. We heard her mum come in down the hall and Janet wanted to show it to her, so I settled down to open my present again. No such luck.

Johnny Ho arrived. And he was, if anything, even more excited than Janet.

Johnny dragged me off to see the Best Free Show in Town, as he called it. I had to keep telling him to slow down, I couldn't walk that fast. He didn't take any notice, just kept running ahead, yelling, "Come on, or it'll be too late!" Eventually I found that if I kept my legs absolutely straight and just swung them, I could move a lot faster, even if it did make me look like a zombie with a bee up his bum.

Luckily, it wasn't far. We turned onto High Street and there it was. I could hardly believe my eyes. Johnny settled himself on a wall, opposite the newsstand, and offered me something from a bag of his mother's weird snacks. I sat down, took one, and we just watched.

And very enjoyable it was too. The whole window of the newsstand was full of copies of the magazine with Paul's portrait of Janet. That wasn't the really good bit though. The really good bit was Daisy Micklepage throwing the biggest tantrum the universe has ever seen. She was in total hysterics, screaming and shouting and tearing up a copy of the mag while her cronies looked on embarrassed and the shopkeeper tried to move her on.

As Johnny said, there's nothing that gives you a healthy appetite more than watching a supermodel make a complete twonk of herself in public.

I practically choked on my foo yung butty.

It was true. My picture WAS all over the Sunday papers. It made me feel a bit weird actually, thinking about my face

being on everybody's breakfast tables and ending up underneath everybody's cat litter. But I was pleased.

Sort of.

I was pleased because I liked Paul and I was glad that I'd helped him (even in a little way) to go back to being a famous artist again. I'd stopped caring (much) about the way he seemed to like Charlie so much more than me. I still didn't REALLY understand why he acted like that (though I have my suspicions, which Mum says I've got to keep to myself or she'll KILL me!!!!!!) — I was just glad that Charlie had found someone who was NEARLY as special to him as Wizzo was to me (because of course nobody could be quite THAT special).

Which must've meant I was becoming a Better Person.

Or else I'd just stopped being so jealous.

147

I've been thinking about jealousy a lot recently and I reckon that just because somebody you really really really really like, really really really really really really likes somebody else it doesn't mean they can't like you as well, does it?
I mean, just because I love my mum doesn't mean I can't love my dad as well, does it? And just because she loves me doesn't mean she can't put up with Dee no matter how much of a pain she is. It's not as if you have just a certain amount of LIKE in your head and it has to be shared out between all the people you know (how much would Daisy Micklepage get? Er, none!). You have different bits of your brain set aside for different people.

And that's how it is with me and Charlie.

I've got a bit of my brain with CHARLIE written on it and he's got one labeled JANET. And just because he's also got a bit labeled

My Brain

PAUL now, it doesn't mean the JANET bit's got any smaller.

D'you see what I mean?

Anyway.

All this thinking about Paul and Wizzo made me feel a bit sad. I remembered about Wizzo having a new girlfriend and that got me all upset again. In fact it got me SO upset that all the stuff about not being jealous went flying out the window. I mean, what if they DID get married and had loads of babies and he forgot all about us? It COULD happen! Then CHARLIE would still have Paul (I BET he gets invited to go and stay with him next holidays, I BET he does) and I'd have NOBODY.

And that started me feeling INCREDIBLY jealous.

So I decided to write to Tiffani (that always makes me feel better). And I thought I'd check my e-mails first.

And guess what?

A new one had arrived.

And it was from my Dad.

I finally got home to my present, but not until the security guard from the shopping center had forcibly dragged Daisy away from the shop.

This time there were no interruptions, and I soon had the parcel open. It was what I'd guessed. A football. Good old Paul. A football with writing on it.

I looked at it more closely. It was signatures. Only the signatures of every one of the French team who won the 1998 World Cup!!!!!!!!

GOOD OLD PAUL!

What a mate! It was the best present I'd ever had. There was a note with it too. It said:

"Score one for me, son."

Which just goes to show how good his English is. I'm sure the French don't go round calling each other son, or mate or pal, or any of those things.

"Score one for me, son," signed, Paul le père.

Excellent.

To: janet
From: wizzo
Re: life etc

hey gorgeous, just to let you know that yr old
man split up with the Girlfriend this week (turns
out she's allergic to Transit Vans! Well, I couldn't
live with a woman like that, could I?) and is
coming to see you as soon as. He needs a big big
cuddle off his best best girl.

Love you loads

Your
mad, sad, bad, dad
Wizzo x

I wasn't jealous of Charlie anymore.

I wasn't jealous of anyone.

I'd had a brilliant holiday in France with my

best mate. I had a portrait of myself painted by a famous artist hanging in my bedroom. And my dad was coming to see me.

Everything was PERFECT.

And it always would be.

Charlie!!!